Prejudice and Pride

Prejudice and Pride

WINIFRED FOLEY

ISIS
LARGE PRINT
Oxford

First published in Great Britain 2005
by
Isis Publishing Ltd

Published in Large Print 2005 by ISIS Publishing Ltd,
7 Centremead, Osney Mead, Oxford OX2 0ES
by arrangement with the author

British Library Cataloguing in Publication Data
Foley, Winifred
    Prejudice and pride.– Large print ed.
    1. Large type books
    I. Title
    823.9'14 [F]

ISBN 0–7531–7223–2 (hb)
ISBN 0–7531–7224–0 (pb)

Printed and bound by TJI Digital, Padstow, Cornwall

Obituaries

Dame Kezzie Clarke

The death was announced last week of Dame Kezzie Clarke, an icon among the famous singers of the 1930s, of whose voice it was said "once heard, never forgotten". Hers was a remarkable rags to riches story. Born in the beautiful Forest of Dean, dire poverty drove her family out of their primitive rented cottage when her father was jailed for theft, and Kezzie and her mother joined a local group of gypsies. During a holiday with his wife, the famous entrepreneur Rudolph Penn overheard Kezzie singing as he walked in the Forest. Amazed at the purity and power of her voice, he persuaded her mother to allow him to take this prodigy to London for training. Penn and his wife gave Kezzie a home and promoted her career to international fame. She finally retired after many years of successful appearances worldwide, moving back to her childhood home of the Forest of Dean. Dame Kezzie Clarke never married.

CHAPTER
ONE

The school stood on a grassy plateau on the side of a wooded rise almost a mile high in the beautiful Forest of Dean. A sturdy stone-built Victorian edifice that blended well with its sylvan surroundings, it housed two teachers and two rooms for the infants and four larger classrooms for the pupils, most of whom left at 14 years old to go into work. Three teachers and the headmaster had the job of getting the three "r"s into far too many reluctant heads among the older pupils. The huge Gothic-style windows were set too high for the pupils to be distracted by anything they could see outside. It had a small walled playground for the infants and a huge area of greensward for the others, with ditches and banks as well as flat areas, a wonderful natural playground!

It was unfenced but no-one ever worried that a child would be abducted or abused — apart from the boys sometimes fighting amongst themselves, the children's world was safe. Save for the Headmaster's house at the back of the school and one nearby cottage that sold sweets, there were no other habitations within sight of the school. But fecundity was rife in the few surrounding hamlets and villages catered for by the school, some 300 pupils filling the school to capacity. Most of the children's fathers were miners, who were working for mere pittances in this time of depression during the late 1920s.

There were few frills to the school — bucket toilets in two rows back to back at the far end of the playground served the pupils, six for the boys and six for the girls. The teachers were allowed to use the Headmaster's private earth-closet, which was in his garden.

The lunchtime break was nearly over. Lunch for many had been wrapped up in newspaper, the lucky ones having a piece of mother's home-made cake. For a few, including Kezzie Clarke and her brothers, lunch had been what other children shared with them from their own small lunches, for their mothers were hard put to it to get any food onto the table each day. Kezzie, a small dark-haired sprite, was playing hopscotch with her bosom pal Tess Avon, who was fair-haired and tall. Three of the teachers were observing the children through the window.

"What a morning I've had! Poor little Nellie Mowbray fainted in class, Timmy Haynes kept putting up his hand to go to the lavatory, and Mary Jones said Sammy Fletcher was pinching her leg. I hardly got through any of the lesson. Sometimes these children hardly seem worth bothering with," said Miss Rawton.

"Oh come, Mavis, that's a bit hard on the poor little creatures. Most of them are under-nourished, under-clothed, live in cottages that are little better than hovels

2

and have mothers struggling beyond hope of giving them a proper upbringing," said Mr Davis.

"And yet there's talk now of their fathers coming out on strike!" said Miss. Rawton.

Mr. Davis replied, "Can you wonder? If I was a miner working in the conditions they do for such inadequate wages and then being faced with a demand by the owners to take 6d a shift less, I would go on strike."

"Well, *I* marvel how well some of the mothers manage. There's quite a few children kept clean and tidy and cottages that inside are a credit to their mothers, with shiny black grates, scrubbed flagstone floors and rag mats shaken every day," joined in Miss. Hill.

"And all the children aren't stupid. I get a very bright one every now and again," said Mr. Davis.

"How I agree with you! That Tess Avon and Kezzie Clarke are both above average where brains are concerned. They are both top in every subject and Tess can draw exceptionally well. It's a shame that when she leaves school at the end of term she has to go into service. Her Aunt Jessie in Bristol has got her a job near her," said Miss Hill.

Mr. Davis asked, "She passed the grammar school entrance with the school exam, didn't she?"

"Yes, with flying colours, but the interview with the school let her down. I fear they would never let a daughter of such a radical as Horace Avon pollute the grammar school. The governors are all strong Tories, shopkeepers and mine managers," replied Miss. Hill.

"I went to a miners' meeting where Avon was the speaker. I was very impressed; the man has a brilliant mind and he struck me as a true idealist. It's not surprising Tess is a clever girl," said Mr. Davis.

"But Kezzie, where on earth did she get her intellect from? She's almost a year younger than Tess but just as bright, and look at the squalor they live in, that tumbledown isolated hovel twice as far to the village well. Sometimes I think the only wash Kezzie and her four brothers get is when they're out in the rain. Now I hear her mother is ill. Just had another baby, a girl this time," said Miss. Hill.

"Look at the way Kezzie is scratching her head," observed Mr. Davis.

Miss Hill replied, "I know, she's lousy, poor child. She acts aggressive and a bit rough, but it's a front to hide her feeling. She can't bear to be patronised in any way."

Mr. Davis looked at his watch "Well, time to go out and blow the whistle to get the young blighters back at their desks."

CHAPTER
TWO

As usual Tess and Kezzie walked home from school together. When they got to Tess's gate, she ran indoors for the yoke and bucket to fetch water from the well which Kezzie had to pass on her way home. Mrs. Avon was just coming in from the garden.

"I'll walk with Kezzie to the well and fetch some water, Mam," Tess called to her mother.

Her mother frowned, and complained, "I do wish you'd keep away from that lot; I shall never get rid of the nits in your hair as long as you play with that Kezzie. Wait there a minute," and she brought out a piece of bread and dripping for both of them, for despite her sharp words, she had a soft spot for Kezzie and never failed to see that she had a bite to eat if there was any to spare.

When Tess got back from the well, "Be a good little wench," cajoled her mother, "and go to the farm for a penn'orth of milk; I haven't got a drop to go in the tea."

Tess knew why there was no milk in the house. When they ran into too much debt with the young man who brought the milk round in a pony and cart, he stopped supplying milk until the debt was paid off. Tess's mother had borrowed a penny from somewhere and handed Tess a jug that could hold a quart of milk. This was a ploy, because usually they had a lidded metal can that held a pint. However, if Rosie, one of the farmer's daughters, served you, she almost filled whatever jug was offered while only charging for the pint.

The shortest way to the farm was through woodland along a path that meant crossing a field. For Tess there was always the dreadful possibility of some heifers grazing in the field. To small Tess any cow without udders was a bull, and if faced with these fearsome beasts it would mean a long detour to approach the farmhouse from the main road. This time she was in luck. There were no animals in the field and it was Rosie who answered the knock on the dairy door, smiling down at the small figure in front of her. Tess loved to look in the whitewashed cool dairy; it was so tidy with its scrubbed stone floor, it gave her a feeling of peace. As usual, Rosie filled the jug almost to the brim.

"Thank you very much," Tess said and thought how the name Rosie suited the pink and white complexion and long fair plaits of her benefactor.

On the way home, she had to walk very carefully not to spill any of the precious milk. Halfway through the woodland a strange feeling came over Tess. Red squirrels cavorted in the oak branches above her, the birds chirruped and there was a faint hum from the myriad of insects that hovered above the foxgloves and ferns carpeting the earth beneath the oaks. Tess suddenly realised this swarming life was completely indifferent to her.

"What am I? Who am I? Why am I?" she questioned in a sudden mood of spiritual isolation. Deep in thought, she nearly tripped over an exposed tree root, stumbled and spilled a drop of milk. This at once brought her mind back to a sense of reality, but Tess continued to feel a bit disturbed, even when Kezzie came to play later in the evening. It was something she couldn't tell anyone about, not even Kezzie or her dad.

The two girls played hopscotch on the hard flattened piece of earth by the cottage gate, then, tired out, they sat on the nearby patch of grass and chattered. At thirteen years old, boys had become a topic of interest. Like all the girls about their age at school, they were both in love with Johnny Browning, a handsome, confident, cheeky-mannered boy, a farmer's son from a farm about one and a half miles from the school. They both realised they didn't have a chance of catching his interest.

"I wonder who we shall marry," pondered Tess aloud.

"I shan't marry anybody," Kezzie said firmly.

"'course you will," argued Tess. "Everybody gets married. When we go to service and save up for some new clothes, the boys will be after us."

Tess found the answer to her fate, trying to understand the arguments her dad and his mates indulged in. Tess's dad had built a make-do workshop on the side of the cottage. Here he and a few of his pit butties got together to put the world to rights. The names Darwin, Ramsay Macdonald, Lenin, the Pope, God, Einstein,

Trotsky and many others were often mentioned, and their thoughts and theories hotly analysed and commented on. Tess would often spend winter evenings sitting on the fender by the makeshift fireplace listening in enthralled fascination. She came to the conclusion that her Dad's admiration for Darwin and Lenin was right. What they were taught at chapel Sunday School seemed more like fables, but Tess held her tongue. She didn't want to miss the chapel treats!

In discussion about their lives and futures, she usually influenced Kezzie to her way of thinking. They daydreamed of becoming film stars like Mary Pickford, Janet Gaynor or Vilma Banky and discussed at length what they would buy for their families if they had lots of money. They would have meat every day and jelly and custard and eat tins of Nestlé's condensed milk with a spoon. Often these thoughts made them so hungry they would pull some grass to chew.

There was always plenty of ways for the children to pass the time, even during the long summer holidays, playing houses and shops, scouring the big holes where the villagers threw their meagre rubbish for things to help round out their imaginary world: a flat stone, a piece of old metal bath and two tin lids made good scales. Often they had to mind their younger siblings, bossing them about in the rôle of mother. Five similar sized stones could be rattled about in a rusty tin until they were smooth enough for games of five stones. Whatever was on hand to eat at the end of day went down into very grateful stomachs.

8

One day they went for a longer walk than usual and found the top of an abandoned mine, where there was a large flat area of concrete, a perfect stage! Tess's Aunt Jessie had sent a parcel in which there had been a frilly-laced petticoat that fitted Tess. To own such a wonderful pretty garment went to Tess's head. She must show it off to the other girls. She decided to put a concert on. She had sometimes been to the Saturday matinée in town when she had managed to acquire two pence. She always went with a friend, Gladys, as Kezzie never managed the two pennies. Tess was very impressed with the image of the ballet dancer at the end of the Pathé News item, and thought that this was the ideal part to show off her beautiful petticoat.

With Kezzie, she gathered as many village girls as she could muster to take to the "stage", where they could manage to make up a dance to perform. She would take her dress off to show off her petticoat. She had a tidy dress her Aunt had sent as well, a blue Magyar shape with a flower embroidered on the front.

It was a glorious evening for Tess, trying to organise the girls into a chorus line, twirling round, showing off her frilly petticoat. They persuaded Kezzie to sing songs they had learnt at school like "Let us haste to Kelvin Grove", "Bonny Lassie", "Madam, will you walk," and a few others. Her beautiful, clear, sweet voice brought her enthusiastic clapping from the other girls. Sometimes the school would put on a concert which would include the children singing, dancing, and reciting poetry. Costumes for it were usually made with crêpe paper, though this could hardly camouflage the dirt on some of the children or their ragged clothes. Kezzie always obstinately refused to do anything to cover her own shabbiness, although she had a beautiful singing voice, so she was excluded from the selected performers. So it was only her own friends who could appreciate her talent.

They were all so absorbed with her songs that before they knew it, the sun went down and it began to get dark. Tess hastily put on her dress and they all ran to get home. It wasn't until she got indoors and into the lamplight that Tess realised she had put her dress on back to front! Whatever would her mother say if she knew! She quickly went into the little back kitchen for a drink of the water kept in a bucket from the well and hastily changed her dress over.

Sometimes when they were on their own, Tess and Kezzie would wonder if fairies really existed, and sometimes Tess had the courage to express her doubt about the existence of God. She found it all so puzzling — at Sunday School they were taught all about gentle forgiving Jesus who let himself be crucified to help mankind, yet God, His father, was very strict. If you sinned, when you died he let you go to Hellfire run by the Devil.

"My Dad don't believe in the Bible," Tess would say. "He thinks it was written by some clever smart-arses so they could get power and take advantage of the ignorant masses. Anyway," she would add, "my Dad's a far better cleverer man than the minister!"

Fairies were a different matter. They could be shown to be real. Tess and Kezzie would make fairy cups from acorn shells, fill them with water from the well, and leave them set around a flat stone in the moss. They knew that the fairies were always grateful for a clean drink. If the water was still there when they checked after school, they didn't give up hope or belief. After all, maybe the fairies had had plenty of nectar to drink that day.

The two girls were never short of chat. Their vivid imagination foretold countless magical scenarios for when they grew up, fed by the tales in books they both read eagerly. In between, they climbed trees, swinging from broken branches, played shops and houses, and when they found a rare harebell growing at the edges of the forest they kept it to themselves. As it got near the end of term, the talk was mostly about Tess's leaving home and going into domestic service.

"When I've been there a year, I shall have a fortnight's holiday. By then," she told Kezzie, "my Auntie Jessie or me will have heard for a job for you."

"I've got nothin' tidy to wear," answered Kezzie.

"Well, your mam will 'ave to do the same as mine, get some things off the pack man. I shall send 8 shillings a month out of my pound a month wages. You can do the same. He'll let her have them if he know he'll get the money."

Just as the small village pub was the Mecca of social life for the men, Chapel was the social centre of the women's lives, somewhere to show off any bit of finery daughters brought home from service, somewhere for the daughters to show off their hard-earned new

11

clothes, and their attraction in turn brought a few of the village lads to add to the congregation.

Sunday afternoons were Bible classes for the children. Kezzie hardly ever attended, saying "it's nothin' but a lot of bull shit!" and Tess, like many others, only went enough to get the attendance marks for the annual children's outing. Mr. Worth the Sunday School teacher was a kindly, nervy sort of man, so Tess was surprised one afternoon when he asked herself with her pals Dolly, Gladys and Lily to stay behind after class. What had they done? He didn't seem cross with them.

"Sit down, girls," he said. "I'm wondering if you would do Kezzie's family a favour. The Almighty in His wisdom has taken her baby sister back to heaven and poor Mrs. Clarke is very poorly. Her legs are all swollen up and she can't walk. They've no money for a proper funeral, so Kezzie's dad has made a coffin for the baby. It would be a kind gesture if you four girls would take it to the church on Tuesday morning. The vicar will be there to bury the poor mite and you won't have to carry the coffin on your shoulders 'cos Kezzie's dad has put rope handles on it. I'll give you a note for your Headmaster to explain why you missed a morning's school. Kezzie's mum won't be able to give you anything to eat, so come straight from the church to my house and my wife will give you a cup of tea and a bite to eat."

So that, thought Tess, explained Kezzie's swollen-eyed, tear-stained face and withdrawn behaviour this last few days, and why her voice got all choked up when she had asked her what was the matter; poor Kezzie. Feeling solemn and important, the four girls said yes.

"Mind and ask your mums, but I'm sure they'll let you," Mr Worth concluded.

The morning of the funeral, wearing black armbands made by Gladys's mother, the four girls walked solemnly the mile to Kezzie's house. Coming from very humble homes themselves, they were all still shocked by the drabness and dirt of Woodedge Cottage. Kezzie's mother looked grey-faced and ill, her two badly swollen legs in contrast to her thin body. An old sack served as a rug on the hearth, and on a scrubbed table top the dead baby lay in her home-made coffin. A few rickety wooden chairs were all that consisted in the way of furniture and paper blinds served for curtains at the window.

Kezzie's weeping mother struggled to the table and bid the girls look at her beautiful angel baby. Kezzie's father put his arm round her and helped her back to her chair, telling her to remember the baby was gone to a far better place. The girls were inclined to agree with him. He put the lid on the coffin and tied it up, so the girls had a rope handle each. A couple of Kezzie's brothers were hanging about outside but there was no sign of Kezzie.

The girls were very solemn, walking the two miles to the church along the practically empty road. They only stopped and changed hands just once for their burden weighed practically nothing. The vicar was waiting for them and assured them God would take the baby into

Heaven even though it was going into a pauper's grave, for it was an innocent.

Outside the church yard Tess exploded, "God should take everybody whether they could afford a proper funeral or not!"

"Shut up, Tess, you could be struck dead for taking the Lord's name in vain," admonished Dolly gently.

Before they left, the Sunday school teacher's wife gave them tea and bread and jam. Then they dawdled through the wood to school, subdued by the morning's events.

CHAPTER
THREE

A few weeks later, the miners had gone on strike, as
had been threatened, and Tess had left school to start
her new life in the city, where she was to be a general
maid. Mrs. Avon, accompanied by her other children,
took Tess to the little station halt a mile away to catch
the train to Bristol. To know that Tess would be getting
regular food eased the heartache of having to send her
from home.

Tess's Aunt Jessie met her at Temple Mead station
and took one handle of the battered but well-polished
little tin trunk containing Tess's clothes. Aunt Jessie was
giving her some caps and aprons for work. On the way
to her job Jessie advised her how to behave to fit into
the slot her fate had ordained: not to speak until spoken
to, express no opinions, clean in the corners and where
the dust didn't show, always answer yes, ma'am or no,
ma'am or ma'am, if you please, when speaking to her
employers, who were two elderly spinster sisters of
good birth, a bit strict and old-fashioned. But, said
Aunt Jessie, the food they provided was good and Tess
would have quite a nicely furnished attic bedroom. The
maid who had left to get married had been with them
for six years, which was a good sign. They had come

from a wealthy family that had come down in the world and tried to hide it.

As her Aunt Jessie chattered on, Tess's spirits sank lower; a bright, opinionated "chopsymouth" herself, with a strong dislike for housework, she was beginning to panic about her ability to cope. When she tied on the streamered servant's apron, she would be tying up her free spirit with them. By the time Jessie left her, taking instructions from Miss Sarah and Miss Amy on her duties, Tess was near to tears.

The house was a very old stone building. The kitchen was a large room, oblong in shape, with a red tiled floor and three windows, the sills also red tiled, each one with a potted geranium. The cooking range stood in a green-tiled alcove with a patterned rug in front of it; a dresser, cupboards, large scrubbed wooden table and five chairs comprised the furniture. It was very clean and there was not a muddle in sight; obviously this was "a place for everything and everything in its place" sort of house.

By the time her mistresses sent her to bed at 10.00p.m., Tess felt totally disorientated after waiting on them at dinner, washing up, turning their beds down and drawing their curtains, all with an air of deference foreign to her nature.

As her Aunt Jessie had said, her attic bedroom was pleasantly furnished with a pretty pink eiderdown and cover, a wardrobe, chest of drawers and wash-stand, with a charming pattern of roses on the wash basin, soap dish and jug. There was a bathroom in the house but Tess thought it unlikely she would be allowed to use it. As she got into bed, she had never felt so unhappy. There was a whole year to pass before she could go home, and now she knew the meaning of homesickness. She envied Kezzie still able to run free in their beloved forest.

She thought oh, how wonderful it would be when Kezzie came to work in Bristol and they could have their half days off together. While Tess was immeasurably grateful that she would have Aunt Jessie's company on her half days off, she was 50 years old, had left her youth behind and had become immersed in the straight-jacket of servility. She was quite content in the nice weather to sit on the downs, watching the people and indulging in a cup of tea and toasted tea-cake. If the weather was bad, it was the cinema and an ice cream.

Once a month Tess went to the post office and sent home ten shillings from her monthly wage of a pound. The extra two shillings would buy her family four loaves of bread, all of which would help keep the family from starving while the strike was on. But however homesick she felt, the thought didn't cross Tess's mind to go back home. She knew that the money she earned and sent home was worth more than herself and her appetite. The strike showed no signs of ending, and she knew that the strain for her parents to keep food on the table must be terrible. She longed passionately for the year to pass so she could get Kezzie a job and they would have each other's company to feed their dreams on.

CHAPTER
FOUR

Even Tess's imagination could not tell her the real state of affairs. Conditions in the village were at crisis point. Shopkeepers were now loath to let the miners' families have even bread on tick, children were becoming thinner and thinner with their eyes filling their faces, men tightened their belts to stop their trousers falling down and the women moaned to each other about their troubles. Isolated from the village, Kezzie's family fared the worst.

One evening Byrom Clarke could stand it no longer. The children had gone to bed whimpering with hunger. After brooding for a time by the fire, he said to his wife Mary in a manner that broached no denial, "I be goin' to kill a bloody sheep, I ben't goin' to let thee and our young 'uns starve any longer."

It was an ancient right in the forest for men born within a certain area to run sheep to feed on the road verges and in any spaces where grass grew between the trees. It would be considered a traitor's act to take a sheep but Byrom Clarke was too desperate to care.

"If you was to be caught, 'twould be prison and nobody 'ould speak to us again, and how could I keep the children fed?" his wife argued.

He snorted. "They don't put themselves out to speak to us now and look how many times the bloody sheep 'ave broke into our garden and ate the cabbages. I be going to 'ave one. I've fetched plenty o' water from the well and I've dug a 'ole in the garden to bury the skin and hooves and nobody'll smell the meat cooking up 'ere, and we'll tell the young 'uns it's a couple o' rabbits I killed chucking stones at 'em."

"But d'you know 'ow to kill the poor animal?"

"No, I be afeared I don't, but I'll stun it with a hammer afore I put the knife in. There's a couple what do lie at night under that oak right by our gate. I'll 'ave one o' them. When I've stunned 'it, you'll 'ave to 'elp me drag it to the side o' the hole, then I'll lay its 'ead on the chopping block and get it skinned and gutted and drop all the skin, head and 'ooves in the 'ole to bury the evidence. Then when it's skinned, we'll get an old sack and carry it indoors, make up a big fire — thank God we can get plenty o' wood round 'ere — then cook as much as you can and hide it till we've ate it all!"

By one o'clock in the morning Byrom thought he had buried all the evidence and a nice lot of the meat was nearly cooked. The smell had penetrated the hungry light sleep of the children. It brought Kezzie and one of her brothers downstairs, clamouring "We can smell meat cooking, we're famished!"

"Yes, we know. I was lucky, I caught a couple o' rabbits. Go back to bed and we'll bring you some up when it's finished cooking."

"It don't smell like rabbit."

"Don't argue! It's rabbit, now get back to bed."

The disturbance woke up the other four, and in less than half an hour six bewildered but delighted children sat up in bed eating warm chunks of cooked meat.

"Thank God I've got summat for them to take to school to eat," sighed a sleepy-eyed Mary in the morning.

It was the custom for the children to eat their lunches sitting on the grass outside in fine weather but indoors in the "big room" in bad weather. The "big room" served for morning prayers, assembly and classroom for class 4. By lunch time that day the rain was pouring down and, warned to be on their very best behaviour, the headmaster allowed them to eat in the "big room". To eat was hardly the phrase, for the pitiful bits of food they unwrapped. Tess's small sister and brother had dried bread apple sandwiches and only one each.

When the Clarke family took lumps of meat out of the "bait" bag their dad normally took to the pit, the smell of the meat intensified the hunger pangs of the rest of the children. It was amazing, that scruffy lot with meat; true, they had no bread, but nobody had meat these days, not even for Sunday dinner.

"Our dad caught a couple o' rabbits," the Clarkes informed the hungry cadgers.

"That's funny bloody rabbit," observed a bully boy before he snatched the meat Kezzie was putting to her mouth. A fight began and before long the furious headmaster was laying his stick on any bits of anatomy on sight. He was a fastidious man about 55 years old, of very short temper aggravated by the failure of his wife to produce a child of their own. He particularly disliked the Clarke family: unkempt, cheeky, a blight over the school despite their clever sister Kezzie, and they bred like rabbits. It wasn't fair, and how come the fight was over meat. He was sure it was no rabbit; it looked and smelled like lamb, and Byrom Clarke did not possess any sheep to graze in the forest.

A few days later Byrom told his wife he would take another sheep. He once more fetched in plenty of water from the well, and set about digging a large hole in the garden, when two uniformed police men approached him out of the forest.

"That's a fine big hole you be diggin' there," one observed.

"It's for the privy," replied Byrom.

"Seems you empty your privy bucket pretty often. Looks like you've dug another hole in the last few days."

"Well, there be a lot of us, mind; it don't take long to fill up."

"You sure you ain't got a dead body buried there, a sheep maybe? You better dig up that other hole to show us if we've been told malicious rumours about you."

In despair Byrom threw down his spade, shouting, "My kids and wife be starvin', we got no work, no money and the baker stopped our bread!"

"That's as maybe, but they be your kids; you and your missus brought 'em into the world, and you can't expect to keep 'em at other folks' expense. I be afeared we got to take you to the police station."

CHAPTER
FIVE

When deprivation and suffering are the norm, pity is a luxury the law cannot indulge in. Byrom was duly tried and sentenced to a year in prison. The Bailiffs were sent to their cottage to sell any assets other than a bed, table and chairs as payment towards the sheep. They quickly discovered that apart from beds, a table and chairs, there was little to sell. A couple of gypsies from a gypsy site nearby bought a wood axe and a pair of old buckets, but very few people from the village bothered to make the walk.

Destitute, the plight of the family brought them to the notice of the poor law authority. The Clarke family had only the workhouse to turn to, and the malnutrition and chestiness of the two youngest boys soon put them in a sanatorium, while the eldest boy of 12 years old was taken in by a local farmer to do live-in work in return for his board and lodgings. The dreaded last resort of the elderly with families unable to care for them or with no families, as well as for the mentally and physically handicapped, the workhouse and hell were synonymous in people's minds. Kezzie said she would run away, it was like going to prison. It gave Mary Clarke a desperate idea.

She went to the gypsies' encampment and offered them what the bailiffs had left, plus a pretty china jug she had hidden from them, if they would take Kezzie, herself and her nine-year old son with them. They would work for the gypsies and learn to make and sell clothes-pegs for them. The old gypsy granny held counsel and the tribe agreed to try the arrangements. For Kezzie the idea of sleeping on the ground under the stars was infinitely better than an iron bedstead in the workhouse.

It didn't take long for the news to get round the village. One of the villagers walking through the forest had seen a double iron bedstead through the flap of a tent and soon put two and two together. Opinions about their plight varied among the villagers. Most of the women were horrified that such a fate should befall them; one went so far as to say she would poison her children and herself rather than become gypsies. Her husband said the Clarkes were only half a notch above gypsies anyway. A few said that at least Mrs Clarke had some kind of life rather than rot in the workhouse.

Soon after Kezzie with her mother and brother moved in with the gypsies, the eldest son of the gypsy tribe, married with three children, moved to another part of the forest. It was all very amicable, and the son called in often with a rabbit or sometimes a pheasant. Mrs Clarke soon found that the gypsies ate better then they had ever done. Apart from selling pegs and telling the fortunes of the purchasers, which often got them something to eat as well as a few coppers, the men were doing seasonal work on any farm within walking distance. Potato picking earned them sacks of potatoes, apple, pear and plum-picking brought bags of each and the money to buy the sugar for the cooking apples. Cleaning out the fowls' cots was rewarded with eggs, and long hours just before Christmas helping to kill and pluck poultry made sure they had some roasted dinners. One of the young lads went every day to chop and saw wood for a farmer's wife, who gave him a daily can of milk. They also lived from the land, roasting hedgehogs, boiling nettles and gathering nuts and autumn berries. In the winter they gathered mistletoe and holly to sell. All the same, there were hungry days in midwinter, and at that time they rested a lot, the men and women assuaging their hunger smoking clay pipes.

CHAPTER
SIX

Time went with leaden feet for Tess, hard at work in Bristol. She had put 365 ticks on a piece of paper and crossed one out every night before she went to bed, looking forward to the day she could go home on holiday after her first year in service. When the year had gone by, it was a very different looking Tess who emerged to go home for her two weeks holiday. Now nearly sixteen and fed regularly, she had grown taller and rounded out beautifully in the right places. Her long brown straight hair was cut in a glossy waved semi-shingle. The navy serge dress from the packman was packed up to give to Kezzie, being replaced by a smart knee-length suit. Pink silk stockings and stylish court shoes completed the ensemble. With a dab of powder on her nose and perfume on her person, a birthday gift from Aunt Jessie, Tess was a sight for sore eyes. A neighbour spotted her walking up the village hill and shouted to the Avons, "Your Tess is coming".

The whole family rushed up the garden path. The pride in her parents' eyes as they beheld this vision would be hard to describe, and her siblings were reduced to awe and adoration of this elegant young lady who was their sister. But for Tess, seeing the abject poverty of her beloved home and the village, heartache was mixed with the joy of being there. After a celebratory meal, she took the little ones out to play with the bat and ball she had bought them.

Next morning, soon after they had gone to school, Tess walked the couple of miles to the nearest little mining town to buy some fancy cakes and extras for their homecoming. Then she was proposing to go and see Kezzie, to show her the newspapers she had brought home for her to write for a job, and to tell her all her news about being a maid and living in a place like Bristol.

The heart of the little town had steep streets, and Tess was just coming out of the bakers when she saw a couple of gypsies carrying baskets of pegs climbing towards her. One was a middle-aged woman, unkempt and dirty with an equally unkempt young girl. Tess looked with disbelief, unable to believe what she saw. It couldn't, no, it couldn't be Kezzie, but it was — and the look in Kezzie's eyes said, "Don't you dare recognise or acknowledge me, I couldn't bear it."

The shock made Tess feel quite faint. She hurried out of town and cried all the way home. Reaching the house, she burst in, crying, "What happened to Kezzie, Mam? I saw her in town with a gypsy selling pegs."

Her mother explained what had happened, saying, "You best forget them Clarkes, love, they'll never get back from bein' gypsies."

To Tess's untried heart, it was like a bereavement. Kezzie had been more like a sister than a friend, and the thought of not seeing Kezzie any more left her desolated, casting a shadow over the rest of her holiday. Her mind continually filled with desperate ideas how could she get Kezzie away from the gypsies, none of which she could see a way to bring about. She returned to Bristol with a heavy heart.

CHAPTER
SEVEN

Having lost all chance of Kezzie as a companion in
Bristol, Tess was miserable. She loved her kind,
unimaginative Auntie Jessie, but she was now in her
sixteenth year and youth needs youth. Having for a year
had wonderful plans, Tess felt her spirit was in a kind of
prison and she grieved for Kezzie's family's downfall.
When her Aunt Jessie went home for her annual
fortnight's holiday, Tess felt the loneliness particularly
keenly on her half-days off, for she had no other friends
to keep her company. On the first one without Jessie,
she went to the pictures after a stint of window
shopping. Though it was afternoon, the cinema's cheap
seats were quite crowded. Tess made her way to a
vacant seat. She was soon engrossed in the romantic
problems of Rod la Rocque and Vilma Banky, two of
the current screen idols.

After a while she felt a strange sensation of
something crawling up her thigh. It took her a horrified
minute to realise it was the fingers of the man sitting
next to her. Flushed, furious and shocked, she walked
out of the cinema in tears. Still physically unawakened,
her idea of men was the romantic images presented on
the screen by such idols as Rudolph Valentino and John

Barrymore. Romance was still what filled her head. Now the ugly head of sex had been raised by the man in the cinema. Oh, if only Kezzie had been there to help her cope, to share the horror. She dreaded the other half-day before Aunt Jessie came back but in the end all she did was window-shop and go to a tea-shop. On her return, Auntie Jessie had news of her own. She had started to walk out with a widower that lived a few doors from Granny. It was obvious, even in someone as homely and undemonstrative as Auntie Jessie, that she was thrilled to have a man friend.

CHAPTER
EIGHT

Three years later, life was moving on. Aunt Jessie was finally leaving her job to get married, she and her fiancé having spent the time saving as much as they could to find their own home. And Tess's beau couldn't wait to marry Tess.

It had been love at first sight for John Mason. When a new postman on his new rounds, Tess had opened the door to sign for a registered letter and the sight of her lovely face framed in her white morning servant's cap and her small waist tied with the broad apron strings had had the same effect as an oasis to a desert traveller. His love-hungry spirit had landed, but how on earth was he to get to know her when the post was just put through the letter box?

Many of the houses he served employed a maid-of-all-work whose first duty of the day was cleaning the front doorstep and brass door-knocker. He thought that if only he could arrange his round to coincide with this maid's early chores, he could find out more about her. It took time but love will find a way, and he was besotted with Tess's looks. Tess gradually became aware of the good-looking young postman who always passed by when she was doing the front. At last, one day, after apologising for treading on the newly washed doorstep, he summoned up the courage to say

"And what day is your half-day off, then?"

"Wednesday."

"Any chance of taking you to the pictures? There's a good film on with Rudolph Valentino."

"I always go to the pictures with my Auntie Jessie who works in Whiteladies Road."

"That's all right, she could come too."

With reddening cheeks and a fast pumping heart, Tess tried to sound casual.

"All right, I'll come."

"What time shall I wait for you?"

"I finish at 2 o'clock. Well, 'bye 'til then." And she hastily retreated back indoors, her face glowing pinkly.

He was blushing as furiously as she was when he walked off, not on Bristol's solid pavements — he was "walking on air". He was 21 years old and going to take the prettiest girl he had ever seen to the pictures.

Coming round to collect Tess on Wednesday afternoon, Auntie Jessie thought the young man waiting at the back door with what looked like a box of chocolates must be waiting for Tess. She also guessed he might be the nice young postman Tess had mentioned several times. He looked a very pleasant young fellow but, like a mother hen, Jessie began to feel the pangs of worry about her unworldly chick. She didn't shy away from acting gooseberry for the evening and found an opportunity in the cinema ladies' cloakroom to warn Tess not to let this young man take liberties. She warned that all men tried it on, even the nice ones, but the girls who kept them at bay got the best ones. At the end of the evening, she did leave them a precious few minutes to say good night and arrange to meet on Tess's next half-day off.

Their courtship flourished. After several months of courting, Tess had nervously taken John home during her holidays. To her delight, her parents quite approved of him and thought Tess lucky to have a young man in a steady secure job but, like Aunt Jessie, advised them to take their time and prepare for the future. She in turn had met John's mother and stepfather, for his father had died when he was a toddler. His mother hadn't married again until she was in her forties. Sadly his step-father was an alcoholic, a splendid man when sober but spineless when drunk and unable to keep a job for long. As a result, to keep the home going his mother worked long hours as a cleaner in the mornings and a washer-up at a restaurant in the evenings. They both liked Tess and were pleased for John but could contribute little materially to help them.

Though the pit strike was long over, Tess's father as one of the leaders had been victimised by the mine owners. He had to manage on any scarce odd jobs within a long walking distance. To save her parents' having any expense, Tess intended to have the quietest, cheapest registry office wedding possible. Although he would have loved to walk Tess in all the finery of a bride down the aisle, John agreed wholeheartedly with her wishes. Between the small amounts the two of them could save, they started to buy their bottom drawer. No more going to the pictures, no more going into cafés.

Tess spent her half days trudging Bristol for bargains. She especially liked Woolworth's — 6d for a saucepan, 3d for the lid, nothing over 6d. She was cross though when she bought some check teacloths for 6d each and then found the identical teacloths in a bargain draper's for fourpence halfpenny. Are any creatures more contented than a pair of birds building a nest? So it was with them, though Cupid has no reservations and pushed them to unbearable limits of self-control.

His parents said they would buy a new mattress for the double bed that John slept on at home as their wedding present. Tess had told her two mistresses she was contemplating getting married. It was not an unexpected inconvenience to them; she had been a good servant, intelligent and very clean in her ways, but obviously destined for marriage. They would be sorry to lose her and they invited her to choose what piece of furniture she wanted from what was stored in their attic. In this way they could provide for a present without going to any expense. Tess was thrilled and very grateful to find a roomy chest-of-drawers. She saw in the newspaper an advertisement from a reputable furniture store offering a dining-room suite and two fireside chairs for a payment of twelve shillings a month for two years. She and John decided they would be able to manage that between them. There would be plenty of low paid jobs available for the unskilled in Bristol that she could apply for when she left her job.

The great question was somewhere to live within their means. They studied the "To Let" columns in the newspapers at John's home where they now spent their spare time, Tess always bringing something to eat as a thank you to her future parents-in-law. They visited quite a few places before finding one that was within their means and suited them both. It was two large rooms in a large old house that had been turned into a tenement. The water supply was from a tap over a little sink on a landing, and they would share the landlady's lavatory on the ground floor. The two rooms were on the first floor, one of which had a gas stove and some shelves. The two large windows of the other room over-looked an area of grass with a couple of trees in it, a boon for Tess who had remained homesick for her beloved habitat, the Forest of Dean. The rent was 12 shillings a week, above which they dared not go. The landlady's name was Mrs. Truelove, which seemed like a good omen. They promised to let her know in a week when they could start paying rent, as they were getting married but Tess had to give notice in her job. Something about the young couple must have touched Mrs. Truelove's heart strings and she said she would wait 3 weeks. Tess gave in her notice, they booked the Registry Office and ordered the furniture. Her parents somehow scraped the money together to visit on one Sunday, bringing a coal box her dad had made, pillow-cases and a pair of sheets, and a bag of useful presents from the neighbours. Aunt Jessie had sent them a magnificent £5 postal order.

Tess grew very beautiful as love and gratitude oozed through her very bones. After the guestless wedding, they went back to John's old home where they had a high tea of ham and salad, with trim and a fruit-filled home-made cake. Then, without appearing to be too anxious to leave, they at last went to their first home which, in their eyes, was a miniature palace.

It was not long before Tess found herself a job as a cleaner in a hostel for young ladies, working from eight o'clock until four o'clock, augmented at weekends working as an usherette in the Bristol Hippodrome. The first time she was addressed as Mrs. Mason she felt as important as someone newly knighted by the King. They were utterly happy. Tess had learnt quite a bit about cooking from her mistresses, a bonus to go with her physical allure for John, and always made sure there was a good meal ready for him at the end of the day.

Alas, Heaven on earth is a very fragile state. When they been married for less than two months Tess woke one morning feeling really ill with nausea. She was puzzled and could not think of anything she had eaten or done to cause it. The thought of food or even a cup of tea was distressing. John had been up at five o'clock to go to work. Somehow she must get to work. At eleven o'clock each morning, it was the practice for Tess to have a break for coffee and biscuits with the cook. This day she couldn't face food and told the cook how queasy she felt.

"I reckon you've fallen for a baby. Have you missed a period?"

The shock of the remark almost made Tess faint. A baby! A baby! Oh, they weren't ready for a baby, they couldn't afford a baby. They had been so careful; only once or twice had passion overcome precaution. Surely, surely this hadn't made her pregnant already, and why was nature so cruel, making one feel sick like this. Somehow Tess got through her work and went home, bewildered and depressed. What would John say?

He got home from his early shift soon after her, bounding up the stairs and taking her in his arms, then stood shocked as she burst into tears.

"What's the matter, darling, have you got the sack? Oh darling, it doesn't matter, there are plenty more jobs about. Is it bad news, is someone ill, darling?"

He could get no answer between her sobs till at last she wept, "It's a baby, we're going to have a baby!"

John was struck dumb at this news, relief and trepidation struggling equally in his mind. He pulled her down to sit on his lap,

"Don't cry, darling, we'll manage somehow, I'll get an evening job to help out."

"But Mrs. Truelove said no children. We'll have to move when she finds out."

They sat for some time, just finding comfort in each other's arms.

"We'll manage somehow," John repeated, "and I'm hungry, so how about my tea."

"I hate food, I've been feeling sick all day, it's terrible. I was going to do you bacon and egg, peas and mashed potatoes but I couldn't face the smell of cooking."

"Never mind, you go and sit in the other room and I'll do it myself. I'll make you a nice cup of tea."

This brought on more tears.

"Oh John, I can't bear the taste of tea. I just want something terribly sour like a raw lemon."

36

"Right then, I'll nip out and get some lemons before the shops shut," and he was off.

It was a terrible pregnancy, with nausea and abnormal food fancies, and they had to move to a dearer tenancy at 15 shillings a week. Their love for each other survived all the tribulations, and Tess eventually gave birth to a six and half pound perfect baby boy, who they named Robert. They were both besotted with their creation, John's mother equally so. She helped them out to the most of her limited resources. It was she who had bought them a pram from the junk shop for half a crown. It had good tyres and body but no hood. Tess bought some oilcloth and fixed a reasonable cover on the rusted frame.

Tess soon found work again as an usherette at the Hippodrome at weekends whilst John and his mother coped with the baby. In the mornings she took odd jobs as a domestic help where she could take the baby in the pram. They managed and felt it was a small price to pay for the happily growing baby. John grew more and more in love with Tess, watching the tender efficient way in which she coped with their son, the way she dished up the excellent meals she cooked for him, and the warm appreciation she showed to his mother.

CHAPTER
NINE

He loved her too much. When baby Robert was five months old, Tess awoke one morning with the terrible nausea that could only mean one thing! She was 21 years old.

The woman who had cleaned the grand entrance of the Hippodrome and the downstairs toilets left the job due to old age. Tess asked the manager if she could have it, saying she would work extra time for the same wage if he would let her bring the baby in his pram. The manager liked Tess and felt pity for this attractive, bright girl tied down so young in life. He agreed.

Feeling sick, weak and ill, Tess struggled to work on. The warm body of her son brought her boundless joy as she catered for his needs while her pregnancy advanced. Shabby, misshapen and worried, Tess was a pathetic figure as she scrubbed the grand entrance of the Hippodrome, the baby near her in his pram.

"You want to tell your old man to tie a knot in it," a sympathetic female passer-by told her.

As she worked, Tess often thought of Kezzie. Poor Kezzie — maybe she was married to a gypsy now. Fancy bringing up a baby in a tent — how lucky she was compared to Kezzie. At least she had a loving husband and a roof over her head.

When her second baby arrived, life became a test of endurance. It was impossible to take two children to work. Somehow, John's mother found a little spare time twice a week to mind them so that Tess could take on a couple of charring jobs. In the evenings John took over their care whilst Tess worked as washer-up and waitress in a fish and chip shop. A couple of times a week, from her meagre earnings, she bought fish and chips for supper. She also brought home the smell of frying oil on her person, clothes and hair.

"I'm married to a regular fish wife," John joked, but upset by the comment Tess gave up the job and found another washing up in an hotel from Monday to Saturday evening. Sunday they kept for themselves. Their special treat was to take the two boys out. John never minded pushing the pram but mostly carried Robert the older boy on his shoulders. Times were especially difficult when the children succumbed to the usual illnesses of childhood. But almost unbearable for Tess was when Robert caught scarlet fever at the age of three and was sent to an isolation hospital for six weeks.

The separation made Tess so upset that she became quite ill. But from then on it was plain sailing — the boys thrived and were happy. The struggle of bringing them up made the bonds between Tess and John even stronger and it became a very good marriage. They were wonderful support for each other when first John's step-father, then Tess's mother died within two years. Both his mother and her father had gone by then as

39

well, but they drew their spiritual, physical and emotional nourishment from each other, and life was still good.

CHAPTER
TEN

The staff at the famous ancient hotel in the heart of the Forest of Dean were not unduly impressed when the well-known impresario Rudolph Penn booked a fortnight's stay for his wife Isabelle and himself. After all, it had started out as a hunting lodge for Royalty, kings had slept here and well-known guests were commonplace. For Rudolph Penn, it would be a working holiday. It was during the summer months of July and August that he organised tours for the artistes on his books, who included such luminaries as Melba and Pavlova. One afternoon, when they had eaten a bounteous luncheon, Rudolph suggested they go for a walk in the nearby woods. Isabelle declined, declaring that a nap was more in her line.

Setting off on his own, Randolph thought how beautiful the forest was as he walked in the dappled sunshine under the magnificent oak trees with their undergrowth of ferns and foxgloves. When he retired, he thought, maybe this Forest of Dean would be the place to settle in. As the pastoral beauty bewitched him, he heard a sound that matched its enchantment and it stopped him in his tracks. It was a female voice of incredible sweetness and purity which trailed off now and again to whistle better than a lark.

He heard someone call out and the singing stopped. For a moment or two he wondered if he was hallucinating, like desert wanderers "seeing" an oasis, then the singing started again and he made his way hopefully to its source. After a bit of meandering, he came across a small clearing where a family of gypsies lived on a permanent basis. There were three tents, with a rope clothes-line hung between two trees where a young gypsy woman was pegging out washing and singing away. She looked surprised at the sight of this stranger and even more surprised when he raised his Panama hat and asked her if anyone had told her what a fine singing voice she had.

"One of my teachers liked my singing," she said

"Did you go to school?"

"Yes, I went until I was nearly fourteen years old. We didn't live here then. We had a house only half a mile from the school."

He wondered what had brought this bright, fine-looking young creature to this situation. His trained eye had noticed not only her grubbiness and skin bronzed by the outdoors and smoke from the fire, but also her fine features and figure. But it was the voice! An expert judge of talent, he thought to himself this untrained young gypsy's voice rated as high as Melba's. Somehow he must get her on his books, but how? It would be a tricky situation to bring about.

42

An old woman sitting at the opening of one of the tents called to the girl, "If the gentleman would like to cross my palm with silver, I'll tell his fortune."

"Is that your grandmother?" he asked.

"Oh no, we're no relation, just living with her family."

"Are your mother and father about?"

"My dad died three years ago and my mother is out till this evening."

Ready to congratulate himself, he put a golden guinea in the old woman's outstretched hand but told her he would rather his future would be a surprise. He had just had a delightful one, he told her, listening to the young lady singing.

"I'm quite a judge of people's talents. I employ artists and put on concerts to promote them. I think it's possible the young lady there might be a suitable candidate. What is her name, by the way?"

"It's Kezzie. We took 'er mother, brother and her in when 'er father was put in prison for stealing a sheep. He's dead now and 'er mother's out selling clothes pegs."

He went back to speak to Kezzie who, having hung the washing out, was sitting on a tree stump whittling bits of wood with a knife to form peg sides.

"I think maybe I could give you a job singing with that voice of yours. I put on concerts and they do very well. You wouldn't have to make pegs anymore."

Kezzie shook her head, disbelieving this toff. She knew what they were like, always after something easy.

She replied "I couldn't do that. I've no clothes to wear for that sort of job."

He laughed gently, saying, "That would be no problem. My wife would fix you up with all the clothes you need. You could pay me back from your wages, and if the public like your voice as much as I do you would soon be able to buy a big new caravan for your mother. My wife and I are staying at the Speech House Hotel. I would like to bring her tomorrow to meet you and your mother."

He took two gold sovereigns from his pocket,

"Please give your mother those as it means she won't be able to go to work tomorrow."

He wondered what sort of mother she had. He was used to dealing with difficult personalities. To get this young girl on his books he would use all the skill and persuasion at his command.

He hurried back to the hotel and was still a bit out of breath when he sat down by Isabelle working on a piece of the tapestry she was forever doing, gasping out, "Oh, Isabelle, you should have come with me; the forest is so beautiful it felt like heaven on such a perfect summer day. Then to cap it all I heard someone singing so sweetly it could have been an angel."

"Calm down, Rudie, whatever are you on about? Have you got a touch of the sun or something?"

He smiled. "Oh dearest, it does seem an odd thing to happen to me, makes one believe in fate, but someone with the loveliest voice started to sing not far from where I was walking. I went to where I thought the sound was coming from and there was a young gypsy girl hanging out washing between a couple of trees. There were three tents there and an old woman sitting by one of them. It was the girl doing the singing and she was whistling like a lark as well. And to top it all, though she was dressed in rags and was dirty, she's a real corker for looks and figure. I could just see her cleaned up in stage gypsy clothes with a woodland background and maybe she could have dancing lessons and that marvellous Yugoslavian young dancer I had last year could do a gypsy dance with her."

"Good gracious, Rudie. For goodness sake, come down to earth before dinner, or you'll be up half the night with indigestion!" Isabelle remonstrated.

"All right, dear, but will you come to see her tomorrow? Apparently her father is dead; they were cottagers but he stole a sheep and was put in prison. The mother chose to take her and her children to live with the gypsies rather than go in the workhouse."

Isabelle was amused and horrified, saying, "Good Heavens, Rudie, you want to watch what you are getting mixed up with!"

"Yes, dear, I realise it a dodgy situation but I've said we would like to meet her mother and discuss the idea with her. Please bear with me, dear, this girl is a real find!"

CHAPTER
ELEVEN

Although two years of living as a gypsy had greatly affected Mary Clarke, she was an intelligent human being caught up in life's poverty trap. She was still able to hold a reasonably thoughtful conversation. Long aware of Kezzie's lovely voice, it never occurred to her that life would give her a chance to use it, and she was very mother-cautious of any dangers for her daughter. However, these people seemed very respectable and upper-class, and the gentleman's offer to provide clothes and anything Kezzie needed, and the lady's invitation that Kezzie live with them in London for a trial month to see if she was suitable to be put on her husband's rota of performers, re-assured her. A jubilant Rudolph Penn left the gypsy site.

An excited, tremulous Kezzie left a week later. In the meantime, Isabelle Penn had astonished the ladies' outfitters in the little mining town by the value of her purchases, the best customer they had ever had! Kezzie kept looking down at her dress and new shoes and touching the bow of ribbon in her hair. But she was still a long way off the figure the Penns aimed to make of her, for Kezzie had still not had a proper bath.

First the taxi to the station, then the long train ride to Paddington; for Kezzie the journey was almost unbelievably exciting. The first-class train carriage was unbelievably opulent to Kezzie, and the never-ending journey with its changing views fascinated her. In turn this quiet, shy, beautiful girl brought many curious glances from the other passengers. She didn't seem quite to fit with the couple she was travelling with. Kezzie kept thinking what would Tess think of all this? She often wondered what had happened to Tess, remembering her with love and accepting that being a gypsy meant they would never be able to mix again.

By the time the taxi dropped them at the Penns' residence in Wimbledon, Kezzie felt disorientated with wonder. The size of the four-bedroomed villa, the luxury of the furnishings and the fact that they employed a cook-general and house parlour-maid as well as a daily cleaner was such a contrast to life in a tent! Kezzie felt like a fish out of water. Sitting at the dining table, being waited on by a uniformed maid, did not make for a comfortable meal, for Kezzie kept wondering what the maid would think if she knew she was only a gypsy. Kezzie was very intelligent and not burdened with a subservient spirit. Kezzie's inexperience nevertheless overwhelmed her impressions.

Over the dinner table, Rudolph was further astonished by this young gypsy's intelligence. He had explained that she would need to have her voice assessed and, if she was suitable, she would have to learn more songs and how to promote a stage presence.

She readily absorbed and understood what his aims were regarding her and said she would do her best.

With great tact Isabelle suggested that Kezzie must have found it a tiring day, so perhaps she would like to take her bath at 8.30pm and have an early night. Peggy the housemaid would help her wash her hair first. Kezzie was amenable to everything these extraordinarily nice people suggested. The wonder of her bedroom with its pink velvet curtains, rose-patterned carpet and fat pink eiderdown, plus a pretty nightdress and the first dressing gown she had ever seen, made her feel nervous. But human beings are amazingly adaptable creatures and she luxuriated, lying in the scented bath of warm water and knowing what it felt like to be absolutely clean for the fist time in her life.

She was worried about the rim of dirt left on the bath and she was greatly relieved to get it off with her new sponge and lots of scented soap. Some of her old self went down the plug-hole with the water. For a while she felt like singing to express her gratitude.

The next day her patron took her to see a music teacher, an Italian of great repute named Boscarelli. Like Rudolph he was very impressed with her voice and ability to understand what was needed of her to properly exploit it.

Anxious that his "find" be groomed for action as soon as possible, Rudolph arranged to have daily training sessions for Kezzie. Boscarelli put Kezzie in mind of a blow-fly, buzzing, over-active and over-emotional about his work about which he was passionate. He scared her at first, often reducing her to tears. She had never heard the word "diaphragm" or thought there were proper ways to breathe and stand. But he gave her so much lavish praise to counteract his criticisms that before long she had ceased to be frightened by him and was enjoying the stimulation and interest of his teaching.

Kezzie knew nothing of romantic love but she had known joy and heartache, and Boscarelli was brilliant at teaching his pupils how to translate emotions into music and song. A man of the world, he also manipulated her movements and stage presence to make the most of her beauty. By the end of six weeks' hard work, Kezzie could sing a saucy song in the most captivating manner or a romantic ballad as sweet and subdued like a lovelorn innocent; she could also be as flamboyant as a passionate senorita. Boscarelli had taught his art well. Rudolph gladly paid him his fee, for he knew he had found a star.

CHAPTER
TWELVE

Incongruously set in the leafy avenue a couple of turnings away from the Penns' villa was a post office. When Kezzie had been with them about a week, Isabelle asked her if she would take a letter to be registered. Kezzie felt very pleased to be asked. "First turning right, then first turning left," Isabelle instructed her. Kezzie found the post office with no trouble and sent off the registered letter. It was when she stepped back outside the office that panic struck her. She could not remember which way she had approached it. To her, all the villas looked similar. She had not taken much notice of any differences. She felt extremely foolish and a little scared. She had never got lost in the Forest, and could always find her way home there, but somehow her instinct failed her. She couldn't ask indifferent passers-by to help because she had not taken notice of the name of the avenue where the Penns lived, though she knew the name of the house was Bella Ville.

She walked a little this way and then tried a turning, but it was no good, she was lost and the tears weren't far away by the time Isabelle came out to find her. It was a topic of amusement at the dinner table that evening, but Kezzie was mortified. She marvelled at London, its size, its variety and its citizens. Just living in it made her feel important. The pavements under her feet had been trodden by the powerful, the great, the geniuses and the evil. Never, when her teachers at school read out some history of London, had she ever thought she would visit it. If only Tess was with her to share its marvels.

Two months later, her initial month's stay had successfully been extended with her mother's agreement. "Just look at her. I reckon we have achieved a miracle," observed Rudolph to Isabelle as they watched Kezzie walk down the garden to hang some nuts by the bird table. It was hard to think this beautiful, elegant girl was the grubby, unkempt creature of a couple of months ago.

"I know, I would love to adopt her. Rudolph, would you consider it?"

"No, no, it's too late, darling. She's a grown-up woman. Her life has been with her mother; it must have made them very close. It wouldn't be right to usurp that relationship in any way, but we'll keep a parental eye on her."

At the end of the next month, Rudolph put her on his payroll. Five pounds a week and her keep seemed a fortune to Kezzie, and she said she would like her mother to have three pounds of it, so that she would be able to move back into a cottage. Rudolph said he would arrange this and promised her much greater rewards if she became a success. By the time a couple more weeks had passed, he had put together a touring programme of a superb Irish tenor, a famous pair of tap-dancers and Kezzie, with supporting acts. Their first tour would be of the West Country, starting in Bristol. Concerned that it would all be successful, he booked himself as well as the artistes into a hotel there for the first week.

Kezzie sometimes felt scared, and Rudolph tried to allay her fears.

"Just shut your eyes and think you are back in that lovely forest and sing just as you did there; and remember, if you do well, you will be able to help your mother and buy clothes and things for your brothers and help them get proper jobs. Sing for them, Kezzie, and at the same time give pleasure to all the audiences. If you keep going as well as you have at rehearsals, we've got nothing to worry about. We'll go to Bristol on Sunday and have a try out at the Hippodrome on Monday so you'll see what it's like it to be in a real theatre."

CHAPTER
THIRTEEN

On a dreary Monday morning Tess dragged her tired body out of bed, while the baby was still sleeping. Her adoration of him made life possible to bear, for now in the sixth month of her second pregnancy she was still feeling nauseous, unable to face proper food or the thought of a cup of tea. She forced some porridge down, combed her lank hair, dressed herself in her dowdy dress, laddered stockings and down-at-heel shoes, putting her overall over her dress, and commented dryly to herself, "God, what a bloody sight you look". Then as the baby started to whimper, she picked him up and cuddled him, letting the warmth from his plump little body permeate her own with the ecstasy of motherhood. With him changed, fed and comfortably placed in his shabby pram, they made their way to the Hippodrome.

She was on her knees washing the entrance steps when a large and opulent car drew up. A distinguished looking man about 50, a younger, stouter one, a foreign-looking young man and girl, and a very elegant young woman stepped out. Tess could smell the perfume as they mounted the steps, and she turned to glance at them. She froze in disbelief — it was, it couldn't be, it

53

was impossible — but it was. The elegant young woman who had glanced down, also in disbelief at what she saw, was Kezzie. The colour she had drained from her face in shock, but Tess's expression beseeched Kezzie not to "recognise" her even if she wanted to. Kezzie understood and her eyes filled with tears. Both girls thought, "Why was life so contrary and hurtful?"

Then the moment was gone as the group entered the theatre. Tess stood up and found she had to hold onto the wall to stay steady; then things began to fall into place. The showbills on the hoardings had been up for a week advertising among the other offerings of the show "The Woodland Lark", a new singing sensation. The teacher at school had often gone on about Kezzie's voice and made her sing in class, but she was never included in the school concert because of her awful clothes and unkempt appearance.

But how could scruffy, nit-ridden, dirty Kezzie turn into such a beautiful, smart young woman? What had happened and were the rest of the family still gypsies? Tess could not sort her feelings out — joy for Kezzie, envy for Kezzie, curiosity and shock, all overwhelmed her. Social strata had parted them and were again keeping them apart. Kezzie was now famous and well-off, Tess was one of the struggling masses of the underprivileged, and good manners demanded the two did not mix. Tess couldn't share the trauma with John; it might make him pity her, comparing her life to Kezzie's, and maybe he would feel responsible for her plight. That she could not allow. Despite her exhaustion, it was a long time that night before she could go to sleep.

Equally shocked and full of concern for Tess, and understanding Tess's need to keep her pride, that night Kezzie's loss of sleep came more over Tess than the worry of her debut on the stage.

She need not have been concerned over the latter! She indeed caused a sensation on the theatrical front, with the critics unanimous with their praise. They raved: "Her voice was like a honeyed bow on the heartstrings!", "Lyrical, makes one believe in fairies!", "A lark indeed!"

The theatre played to packed houses for the rest of its month's run. Kezzie's future was assured. Rudolph Penn was full of self-gratification. But it was a relief to Tess when the month was over, for she had dreaded another encounter with Kezzie. They were two spirits from a similar mould, not strong enough to fight the face value of convention, so that each suffered for their weakness. Each went their way, diminished by the loss of the other.

CHAPTER
FOURTEEN

Four years later, at the age of 25 years old, Kezzie was enjoying a very successful career with masses of public adoration, but one which left little opportunity or any overwhelming desire for relationships with the opposite sex, damped still further by the parental attitude of Rudolph and his wife. That was, until James Mallinson came on the scene. A noted and handsome young Yorkshire baritone that Rudolph had been very keen to get on his books, for Kezzie he was a true revelation, the personification of her ideal male. A little short of six feet in height, he was a broad-shouldered, well-built young man. His squarish, attractive face was crowned with thick brown hair, a cow's lick parting over his forehead. It was his eyes, dark blue and pools of kindness and tenderness, that first drew her attention, but it was not long before she was totally smitten with the sound of his voice together with his looks. She had fallen suddenly, unexpectedly and completely in love, and was far too naïve to hide her feelings.

Kezzie herself had grown into a graceful, well-formed-five-and-a-half-feet-tall, elegant young woman, with long-lashed, big, lustrous brown eyes, a neat straight nose and a kissable mouth, supported on a slender neck and crowned with long glossy dark hair. She was also still very young and naïve, and her feelings for James soon made themselves very clear as she gazed at him whenever they were near. It would have been an odd male not to be aware of her admiration and James was only human. At 27 years old a man is not a demi-god as Kezzie thought.

The company were doing a two-months' tour of the towns of the South-East and Kezzie blossomed into an outstanding beauty, fed by her infatuation for James, who seemed to return all her feelings. He was soon courting her assiduously and it did not occur to her ever to wonder about his life before they met after he gave her the first kiss. Less than a month into the tour Kezzie had lost her virginity to him and thought she had found the meaning of life.

She was in love with a capital L. She let it sweep her along, blind to any pitfalls. But there is always a serpent in Eden. One fateful Sunday, the cast had just finished their lunch when two women walked into the hotel dining room, one a middle-aged beauty followed by a younger edition of herself. Eyes sparkling, arms outstretched, the younger one ran up to the table where James Mallinson was sitting, putting her arms around him and kissing him as he rose up from his seat by Kezzie, completely surprised and with the colour draining from his face.

"Oh, darling," the girl cried, "Did you think I'd forgotten your birthday?"

The colour came back in his face with a vengeance, and he blushed a deep red.

"My fiancée and her mother," he said lamely to the cast and ushered mother and daughter out of the dining room.

"Kept that up his sleeve", "Sly young dog", "When the cats away, the mice do play", were some of the comments directed at Kezzie, for their affair was common knowledge among the cast. She ran to her room in an utter state of shock and disbelief. She wanted to die! But worse was to come.

It was not long before she realised she could be two months pregnant. In her delirious happiness, it had not crossed her mind this would happen, and in any case it had not unduly worried her, for she had believed that James loved her alone and that they would eventually be married. It was the middle-aged Yorkshire chambermaid, Fanny, that found her weeping with a box of aspirins in her hand.

"Eh lass, what up wi' thee? 'Ast thee lost somebody?"

Kezzie shook her head.

"'Appen theest still got thy tongue as you can tell me. Mebbe I can 'elp thee. I noticed thou's bin lookin' proper poorly lately. Cum on, tell Fanny what ails thee, lass."

"I think I'm going to have a baby," she sobbed.

"Dost the fella know?"

"No!"

"Well, thou must tell 'im, lass, a bit quick."

"I hate him, I'll never speak to him again. I didn't know he was already engaged to someone else!" she wailed.

58

"Eeh lass, men ne'er say no to the chance of an extra woman. They canna 'elp themselves, I reckon."

"Well, I can't have this baby and I don't know what to do. Rudolph Penn will sack me, and he and his wife will never forgive me."

"Well, I'll tell 'ee summat, lass. I've 'ad five bairns and I was just finishing bringing up the last 'un when I fell again, 48 years old I was. I couldn't face it and I was a poor carrier, sick for months wi' all of 'em. Anyroads I was told of this woman who could 'elp me out. She's a reet good sort, an ex-nurse who feels very sorry for women. She put me to rights again. I was only poorly for a couple o' days and none was any the wiser and I 'ad a reet job to make 'er take thirty shillings. That were a time back mind and mebbe knowin' you're who you are and not short of a bob or two she might take more off you, but d'you want to go and see her?"

How she had grabbed at this chance, and sure enough, she was only ill for a couple of days, enough to stay in bed during the day but managing to get through her evening performances. Fanny was so good to her those two days, bringing her food and waiting on her. She made her take some reward and paid the ex-nurse generously for her services.

The experience had also brought a new dimension to her voice.

"No-one can interpret in song the agony of rejected love like Kezzie," one critic observed, "She sings with exquisite pathos and even brings tears to the eyes of a hardened old man like me."

But it also hardened Kezzie's heart against any advances from men in the future. Her ego had been boosted by the public's adoration and the hurt went all the deeper because of it. And oddly, she had never lost a feeling of mourning for that murdered embryo. Oh, how she longed for a confidant to share her feelings.

CHAPTER
FIFTEEN

Heartbroken and disillusioned as she was, the rumours that Britain was on the verge of war with Germany again did not at first register its full horror on Kezzie. The Penns had not known how far her relationship with James Mallinson had gone, but they had been aware of her infatuation with him and made allowances for her miserable behaviour. Like the rest of the country, they listened with heavy hearts to the declaration of war.

Their hearts were even heavier when the government announced all places of entertainment would be closed down for the duration. George Bernard Shaw, the famous Irish playwright and wit, pointed out forcefully what a stupid gesture this was, that it was now more than ever that the populace needed distraction from their worries. The law was quickly changed.

There was still plenty of work for those of Rudolph's artistes that were not called up or had joined the forces, but he had started to worry about Kezzie's lack of verve and decided to have a chat with her. Kezzie, who felt no horror at the thought of being bombed — to die seemed a good idea — thought Rudolph was going to sack her and asked him if that was what he intended.

"No, no, of course not, Kezzie my dear, but Isobel and I have noticed your heart is no longer in your singing. We know you have had a blow to your pride and your feelings, but sooner or later, and it's mostly sooner, everyone gets their hearts broken. I did as a young man. When I was deceived by a girl I was besotted with, I thought my life was over. It seemed to have no meaning. It took time, but thank God I met Isobel, and we have a wonderful, enduring marriage. You are young and beautiful, with all your life before you. Don't judge all men by one of them, Kezzie, and remember always that you have the gift of that wonderful voice, the means of giving such pleasure to people. God knows they need it now. And, Kezzie, you owe it to me and Isobel too. We don't know what this war will bring or how many of us will survive."

By the time he finished, Kezzie's head was in her hands and she was weeping. Rudolph knelt down beside her and put his arms round her.

"You know, Kezzie, Isobel and I have not been lucky enough to have a family and we both love you like a daughter. We do understand how you feel, but try for the sake of everyone, but mostly yourself, to put the past behind you and treat your audiences to the pleasure you know you can give them. Think of how you are helping your mother and brothers. It's thanks to you that they have a proper house. Don't let them down or the audiences that love you too. Don't throw it all away."

Rudolph's kind words did nothing to alter Kezzie's disillusions about romantic love, but it motivated her to

62

be ambitious and concentrate on her career. She thought, "To the devil with James Mallinson and his sort". She would become rich and famous and help her family. That night the intensity in Kezzie's singing brought her encore after encore.

The war dragged miserably on, rationing getting tighter, air raids more frequent, and before long the problem of the morale of the overseas troops came to the fore. A film producer named Basil Dean organised the Entertainment's National Service Association, E.N.S.A. for short. However, Basil Dean at first employed quantity rather than quality and at times the soldiers called the offerings "Every Night Something Awful". Nevertheless, it was not long before he was taking on such luminaries as Grace Fields, Joyce Grenfell, Tommy Trinder and other leading stars. Rudolph thought it would be an excellent opportunity for Kezzie. Her renderings of the lovely old ballads were exceptional — just right for men in the war zone to enable them to indulge in the relief of nostalgia. He obtained a lucrative contract for her with Basil Dean, and Kezzie entered a two-year period of vastly varied experience which left indelible memories.

Life became a concentrated kaleidoscope of places and impressions. She had expected to be in danger, short of food and reasonable accommodation, but they were always far enough from the battle zone to be in less danger than the people back home. Taking advantage of the produce of whatever country they were in, the organisers provided plenty of food. And with her background, a shortage of bathing facilities and a tent to sleep in never worried Kezzie.

Mostly they stayed in hotels. Kezzie couldn't understand why some of her fellow artistes, chiefly the lesser known and more mediocre ones, had the nerve to grumble. She felt that they were only too lucky to have a roof over their heads, beds to sleep in (clean or not), and food to eat. Her own morale was kept high by the wonderful responses she got from her audiences and, despite her poor opinion of the male sex, sometimes a feeling of pity akin to love came over her for the sea of faces of those bewildered, lonely young soldiers. Transport was varied: creaky planes, army truck and Jeeps, on a rare occasion a limousine from an embassy. She saw squalid poverty, grandeur, incomparable scenery and experienced the misery of riding through the desert dust storms in a jeep.

Sometimes the harrowing visions of the day gave her sleepless nights. The wounded from the front were housed in makeshift hospitals with skilled nurses and equipment. If the injuries were not too severe the wounded were relieved and couldn't wait to get posted back home. But one ward was to haunt her for the rest of her life. This one contained those with injuries that were brutal to see, most of the men being maimed beyond repair and some obviously dying. Yet it was here that Kezzie fell in love for the second time. A young officer sitting up by his bed had lost his left leg from the knee down and part of his right foot. Just as with James Mallinson, Kezzie felt an overwhelming attraction for this man. He had the same type of looks as Mallinson, and there and then she had the desire to take this grossly injured man, make a home for him and care for him for the rest of his life. The madness of her thoughts brought a blush to her cheeks. The young man blushed too, for he had also felt a strong attraction for Kezzie. Asking a nurse to fetch a cup of tea for them both gave Kezzie a chance to control her fast-beating heart. They chatted for quite a while and by the end of the visit Kezzie knew his name was Nicholas Burke, and she had his address in Bournemouth and a plea from him to write when she had time.

Though Kezzie had limitless admiration from her audiences, she ached to love and be loved on a personal basis. She waited a month, surmising Nicholas would be back in England by then. No longer able to wait, she could not resist the urge to write and ask him how he was getting on. It was six weeks before the army postal system caught up with her, and when it came it was a letter from his father. Nicholas had died on his way home to England. Kezzie wept and grieved for him and her lost dreams.

Ever after, had the tears that rose in her audience's eyes when she sang a sad song been put together, they would have made a little waterfall. Once again Kezzie turned her back on her own longings and needs, and concentrated on her career, settling for the life of a spinster. Travelling with ENSA brought plenty of distractions and a glimpse into the life of other groups of society. There was a memorable tour when she was in the same group as Tommy Trinder the famous comedian and Joyce Grenfell, another luminary of the stage. Joyce Grenfell had been born into a moneyed and sophisticated world, and socially mixed with famous and titled people. She travelled with her own pianist, Viola Tannard, and often received invitations to the embassies in foreign countries. They once took Kezzie with them.

The opulence of the embassies, the food, the way it was served, and the richness and the variety of the women's dresses, their trivial talk about fashions and gossip flabbergasted Kezzie: all this with a war going on! What would they think if they knew an ex-gypsy was a guest? She had a very high regard for Joyce Grenfell, a woman of great heart and concern for the troops, and generous in spirit. At one concert they put on in a huge tent packed with soldiers, Joyce Grenfell had a very warm reception for her witty monologues. Tommy Trinder, a bundle of matey charm and lewd witty jokes, got an even greater response. But when Kezzie sang four popular ballads, one each for Scotland, England, Ireland and Wales, finishing up with Home, Sweet Home, the clapping and encores nearly brought the tent down.

There was not a trace of jealousy in the way Joyce hugged and congratulated her for the pleasure she had brought the men. A lady by birth and a lady by nature, Kezzie thought.

At long last the war ended. Rudolph, recognizing that she had worked long and hard, bringing her near to exhaustion, made her take a month's holiday. Kezzie spent it with her mother, using most of her time walking for miles in her beloved Forest of Dean. She constantly wondered about Tess.

CHAPTER
SIXTEEN

For Tess, just as life seemed to be going well with both boys growing well and John in a steady job, a terrible shadow came on the horizon which trivialised her daily worries. After much negotiation back and forth, and despite the Prime Minister's much vaunted claim of "Peace in our time", there was increasingly talk of another war with Germany. Due to her father's influence, her own intelligence and her humanist outlook, Tess regarded war as the worst obscenity of human behaviour. She was well aware that noble motives were used to mask the real causes of the conflicts. Her very early childhood had made her fearful of the words Kaiser and German — now "Kaiser" had been replaced by "Hitler", a strutting, almost comical figure running German politics.

As long as Russia seemed to be the target of this dictator's ambitions, Britain had placated him, even supplying him with materials to make arms, but when his territorial ambitions turned westward, and as his troops marched further into peaceful neighbouring countries, the hackles of the powerful of Britain began to rise. It was a source of wonder to Tess how the ego of one human being could influence the masses to cauldrons of hate in one country which aroused equal animosity in another and caused them to kill and destroy each other. What had human beings been given brains for?

Tess felt bitter and sad about it all but she was determined to do her utmost for her family to survive. It was clear that she must be as detached as she could to the evil around her. She knew John was fundamentally anti-war and intended using her considerable influence to persuade him to become a conscientious objector. She felt she could not share her bed with a man who killed his fellow men. They talked about it long and hard. John had the male instinct for aggression in his genes but he compromised. He agreed he would register as a conscientious objector but that he would volunteer to be a stretcher-bearer in the medical corps.

Despite all the rumours and talk, the war seemed slow to start. After the emergencies of the phoney war, the initial terrors in everyone's hearts began to wane. But then the ponderous dragon began to move forward into action, with all its dreadful side effects for people. Once again windows were blacked-out so that night bombers would not target towns and cities, rationing was brought in for food and clothing, and there was always the fear of being bombed or invaded. Tess's nerves grew permanently taut, dreading the idea that her children would be buried by a bomb and that she and John would be unable to get to them.

For the unscrupulous, the black market flourished. Despite all care taken, enough good food became so difficult to obtain that Tess found it impossible to feed her boys adequately. She did her best, but she and John both suffered as she made sure the boys had enough nourishment, keeping herself and John short. John came out in multiple boils and she had anaemia. She hated the black market and those that operated it, but had to admit to herself that she had to sell the clothes coupons she couldn't afford to use in order that the family could have enough on the table.

In due course, John was called up and did as he and Tess had agreed, but to their surprise he didn't pass the medical. The doctors revealed that he had a heart murmur. Relief was overshadowed with worry for Tess, but John made light of it, pointing out that he had had a great-uncle who lived to 83 years old with a hole in his heart. He felt fine, no need to think about it. He was ordered to stay in his postman's job till the end of hostilities.

Tess did any peaceful odd job that came her way. Amongst them was working two weeks as a daily cook for a consultant and his wife whilst their cook was on holiday. She was absolutely astounded by the abundance of food there, a floor to ceiling cupboard in the huge kitchen being stacked to capacity with sugar, tea, pulses and tinned food, and a large refrigerator seeming stuffed with butter, bacon, cheese, meat and fish. Only a week previously Tess had been given three precious cooking apples and had wept because she hadn't enough fat to make pastry for a pie. The highlights in those bleak war years were when Tess's parents managed to visit them, bringing vegetables and fruit from their garden.

At long last VE-day came, bringing a wave of exultation that it was over and that normal life could now restart. Tess and John were so grateful and relieved to have survived with their health and family intact that Tess compared it to herself like the feeling she had felt after she had given birth and the pain was over, a feeling too overwhelming to express.

CHAPTER
SEVENTEEN

One morning, as soon as she woke, Kezzie felt disturbed. When memory came back, she knew why. It was time to take stock and make decisions about what way to spend what life she had left. Here she was, 62 years old, in New Zealand, with no roots firmly settled anywhere. She had retired officially at 60 years old, her voice definitely on the wane, though her technique to camouflage it was very good. Invitations to sing had still kept coming but this tour of New Zealand was definitely her last and now it was over.

New Zealand had always been her favourite venue. Unlike America, where she had never fully been appreciated, or Australia, where audiences were rougher, it was a gentle country, with people who appreciated the way she sang. But England and especially the Forest of Dean still tugged at her heartstrings.

Besides, two of her brothers still lived in the Forest, though no longer as gypsies. Thanks to her, they had houses to live in and a thriving greengrocery shop between them. For many years, until her mother had died, in the short period between engagements she had stayed with her in the cottage she had bought for her.

She had also paid the fare for her other two brothers to emigrate to America. It had still left her with plenty of money for a comfortable, long old age, but if her purse was full, her life seemed empty: no husband, no children, no special place to call her own.

As the thought of husband and child crossed her mind, her mouth twisted bitterly and a tear came in her eye. She blushed too, remembering her humiliation at the hands of James Mallison. It was no comfort that his marriage had only lasted a year, and that he had had a string of liaisons afterwards that did his reputation no good. And despite all that fame, glory and wealth, she had never had any real friends except Rudolph and Isabelle, and they had both died some years previously after Rudolph reluctantly retired at the age of 81.

A terrible sense of loneliness made Kezzie feel very tired. She sat down on the bed and her mind went back to her childhood, Tess, and the beautiful Forest of Dean, and her heart ached for affection and company. Lying in her comfortable bed, she realised that she had never really left the Forest, and that in the end that was her home and her family. She sat up, revitalized by her decision that it was time for her to go home.

CHAPTER
EIGHTEEN

There was an aura of sadness about the woman in black clothes walking up Whiteladies Road in Bristol. She looked in her sixties and had obviously been a beauty in her time, but her kind eyes had a world-weariness about them and her gait was slow and without a firm purpose. Her thoughts mirrored the impression she gave, for this was Tess and her heart had been broken three years previously. Until then Tess had faced her own spurs and arrows of outrageous fortune with courage and commonsense, especially the loss of her and John's parents. During her fifties she was a very contented woman and considered herself remarkably lucky. She had a husband she loved dearly, two wonderful sons Robert and Jim, both of whom had gone to Technical College where they had got good qualifications, Robert the eldest as an electrician and Jim in carpentry. They had married two nice Bristol girls who were like daughters to her and got on together as well as sisters. They had given her and John three grandchildren, a daughter Amy to Robert and Beth, and two sons James and David to Jim and June.

Thanks to Tess finding work at a pastry shop and John's regular wage as a postman, plus help from the

74

boys when they started work, they had been able to buy a house at the end of a short terrace. Being on the end it had a large garden which had become John's hobby and delight. How he loved it when passers-by stopped and complimented him. His large compost bin artfully camouflaged behind a trellis of Japonica was his treasure trove, and as well as glorious displays of flowers, he grew salads and vegetables. They had a good standard of living and were able to be generous to their grandchildren and spend a lot of their spare time with them.

Tess was grateful and envied no-one, not even Kezzie when she read comments in the press about her successes in concerts as far away as New Zealand, Australia and Europe. Tess and John had ideas of maybe going to France for a holiday when John retired, for as a government employee he would have a small pension at 65. He also intended to do odd jobs to boost their income. Small wonder then, that three days before his 64th birthday, with the cake already cooked and hidden at Robert's and his birthday surprises waiting for him there, when Tess woke up in the early hours to find John lying dead beside her, the blow was more than she could bear. There had been no warning. A bit of indigestion now and again was all John ever complained of.

The night previously, before they went to bed, he had been discussing plans of having a small greenhouse at the back of the house. Usually he had his bath and went to bed first but a football match he wanted to watch on the television had kept him up. She was still reading when he eventually got in beside her. She always liked the window open a bit, but the evening air was cool and John gave a little shiver.

"You sure you're warm enough, darling?" he asked.

"Snug as bug in a rug," Tess laughed, putting out her bedside lamp and laying her book down beside it. As she lay back against her pillows, she started thinking of more plans for John's birthday. He was one of those lucky people who dropped off almost as soon as their heads touch the pillow, and he was soon snoring gently beside her.

As with many older people, Tess's bladder made her get up at least once in the early hours. Before she got out of bed, she noticed how cold John's arm felt where his pyjama sleeve had rolled up. She switched on the light to tuck the eiderdown round him, but John had gone. His body lay there undisturbed but his eyes stared out unseeing into that journey from which no traveller returns. No! No! her spirit screamed as she ran bare-footed in her nightdress to wake her neighbours. It was not long before the alarm was raised and soon Robert, Jim, the doctor and the undertaker were there to make this living nightmare real.

If there was a power that kept an eye on our fate, what had she and John done to deserve this? If there was no power or logic in life, it seemed pointless. Only the love she had for her sons and grandchildren and their tenderness and patience towards her gave her the will to survive. She longed for Kezzie to talk to, to unburden her distress, to share her torment and understand. Kezzie was a kindred spirit, but Kezzie lived in a different world. She wondered if Kezzie was married; it had never been mentioned in the press.

Suddenly her thoughts and progress were halted by two strong arms warmly hugging her in the middle of the pavement.

"Why, Robert," she exclaimed, "whatever are you doing here this time of day?"

"Looking for you, Mother. I've got some wonderful good news."

"Is it Beth? Is she pregnant again at last?"

"No, Mum, it's not Beth; wish she was! But it's marvellous news just the same. Mum, I've won the pools, the jackpot, Mum, over a million pounds!"

"Never!" Tess gasped.

"It's true. I've had it all checked. I've got the jackpot. Lucky I signed the coupon to say I wanted no publicity. It's a big thing to happen, Mum, and will take a lot of thinking about."

"I should think it will! My son a millionaire! Are you sure?"

"I've had the day off work and been to the pools office. It's confirmed all right."

"Whatever does Beth say?"

"I haven't told anybody yet, only you. I want to talk about it and ask your advice."

"Oh Rob, if only your Dad was still alive —"

"I know, mum, but you ran the ship in our lives and I want you to help me 'do right' with this money."

Tess's heart swelled with love and pride; a shaft of happiness found a crack in her misery!

"You see, Mum, I'm a bit wary about it 'cos there's a chap I work with who won't even do the pools because of what happened to his cousin in London some years ago. He was a milkman, married with one little daughter, up at 5am every morning and his wife worked in Woolworths, a proper Cockney family. Well, he won over a million on the pools and it ruined their lives. Of course he was over the moon at first to give up his job, then they upped sticks and bought a big posh house at a place called Harrow and sent their little girl to a classy private expensive girls' school. They soon got homesick for their old friends and neighbours and tired of having nothing to do. They would come back in their big flash car to see their neighbours in the pub. He found if he treated everybody he was a big-headed show-off; if he didn't, he was a mean bugger. Their old friends dropped them because they couldn't do the spending and they were like fish out of water with the sort of folk who were normally used to wealth.

"After a couple of years of being rich, they both said they wished they had never won the pools. It's made me think, Mum. I shan't tell Amy how much I've won and I shall tell Jim not to tell his kids. It's altogether 1 million and 10 thousand pounds. I've made up my mind to give Jim a quarter and you a quarter and keep the other half myself. That way you two won't feel beholden to me and I shan't feel too greedy. And I shall put the ten thousand to a good cause in Dad's memory."

"Oh son, whatever do I want all that money for?"

"You could go on a cruise, buy yourself a new place to live in and some real smart clothes. What would you like just for yourself, Mum, money no object?"

"I think I'd like to get a place back in the Forest of Dean, near to the members of my family that are still alive and because I love the Forest, and you and Jim and your families could come and stay and I could have the children in the holidays."

"Right, when things are sorted out, I'll take you back to the Forest to look for the house you want. Now let's go to your place for a cup of tea and a piece of your sponge cake, then I'll go home and put Beth and Jim and June in the picture."

CHAPTER
NINETEEN

Tess's face lit up as Jim tapped her window before letting himself in. He was carrying a sheaf of leaflets.

"Here you are, Mum, Robert asked me to drop these in. They are from some estate agents in the Forest. He wants you to have a good look and choose whatever house takes your fancy. He'll pick you up tomorrow morning about half past ten."

Tess jumped up to put the kettle on, her face flushed with excitement mixed with worry.

"I can't get used to the idea of all this money, and I do be afraid Robert will give too much away and not plan for the future," she said as she bustled about putting out the tea things and looking for something to eat with it. Jim leant back in his chair, smiling at his beloved mother.

"Don't you worry about our Robert, Mum, he's got his head screwed on the right way. A million is an awful lot of money, he has the right to spend a bit lavish, but neither of us are going to be idle. Robert and I will set up businesses for ourselves; pity to waste the skills Dad and you worked so hard for us to train for. But we won't be tied to bosses any more and it will be something to leave to the children. Take it in good heart, Mum; it will give Robert such happiness to see you cheer up a bit."

Tess sat down with a sigh.

"All right, son, I'll do my best. Here, drink this tea up whilst it's hot."

Jim leant forward and put his hand on his mother's, saying, "And don't think because you're rich, Mum, that you've got to stop making cakes for us. This coconut sponge is scrumptious."

Well, thought Tess the next morning as she put on the new navy suit, expensive white silk blouse and navy court shoes, money doesn't give you happiness, but it certainly does make you look a lot better. And she stepped into Robert's new Rover car almost feeling she had a right to! As they drew near the outskirts of the Forest of Dean, her eyes began to mist over and her chest felt tight. Childhood memories came back loud and clear: the poverty, the beauty and freedom of such a habitat, her parents and other loved ones now gone, and Kezzie. Who in a million years would have forecast fame and fortune for Kezzie! Reality had surpassed the wildest of their daydreams.

From the housing brochure Tess had chosen a small modernised cottage not far from the village of her birth. Robert was doubtful about its suitability, but was willing to go along with his mother's evident desire to go home. He demurred, "We'll go and see it but I'm sure it's much too small, no bigger than the one you've got, Mum, so how will you put up Jim and me and our families for the holidays you promised us in the Forest?

81

You can afford a much higher price; besides we shall expect a high standard of accommodation now, you know!" And he laughed at her expression. Eventually, she agreed that perhaps she ought to look at something a bit bigger.

The estate agent was extremely obliging and when Robert told him the figure they were prepared to pay he became positively obsequious!

"I may have just the place for you on my books, sir. Hudson and Son, the best builders for miles around, have built a pair of beautiful Georgian type houses at the edge of town, just over the crest but with magnificent views. On a clear day you can see Gloucester Cathedral. In five minutes you can be walking through the forest footpaths or among the shops in town. One of them has already been sold, but the other one is still on the market. They both have quite large gardens, perfect for landscaping. The one has already been done. I have the keys if you and madam would like to go and view it now."

"It's my mother here who is looking for a house, and yes, we would like to have the keys to see it."

Sure enough, just over the crest of the hill where the town ended, in a very enviable location there were two beautiful houses, each surrounded by a good-sized plot of garden. One had curtains in the windows and cheerfully planted flowerbeds, but there appeared to be no-one at home. Robert as well as Tess were impressed by the interior of the other house with all its modern conveniences, while its size and its Georgian-style sash windows gave it a gracious air. However, altogether Tess felt reluctant. She could not see how she could live in such swank. How could she get accustomed to living in such grandeur? And she made up her mind to turn it down.

As they went outside, a car drew up at the other house and a well-dressed elderly woman got out. Intending only polite smiles, they looked at each other, then both gave ecstatic screams of delight.

"Kezzie!"

"Tess!"

"Oh no, oh my God, this is too wonderful!" and they were in each other's arms, both crying unrestrainedly.

"Come in, come in and have some tea with me," said Kezzie and they followed her into her luxuriously furnished lounge. Tess went into the kitchen and helped put out the cups and plates.

"Are you going to buy the house next door?" Kezzie asked.

Before Tess could answer, Robert chimed in, "I'm sure she will now!"

Jim and he had often been told about Kezzie and how she went to live with the gypsies, then had become a famous singer. Now here they were, two elderly women with 40 odd years of memories to share and recall. Dear old Mum, he thought, it was the best thing that could have happened for her.

He noticed the newspaper in the magazine rack, picked it up and settled down in an armchair. He wouldn't be driving back to Bristol just yet!

CHAPTER
TWENTY

Money may not actually talk but it certainly helps things along. Six weeks later Tess had moved into her new house, with new furniture to replace most of that from her old home. Knowing Kezzie was next door was a priceless comfort to help her adapt. They often sat up late together with some Horlicks, but still Tess managed to get very little sleep. How luxurious her bedroom seemed and what a view there was from its windows, but with her gratitude for all her good fortune came the terrible heartache that John could not share it with her.

The convenience of a bathroom with hot and cold running water, not to mention the modern fitted kitchen with all its wonderful new appliances, made her almost panic with their opulence. But even these were less frightening than the elegance of a dining room with its beautiful polished table. She would make herself a cup of tea and some toast, and sit with them at the kitchen table, feeling more at home there.

One morning Kezzie had asked her to come to her at about eleven for coffee. Kezzie had slept in late and was still in her nightdress and a luxurious silk dressing gown, something Tess had never owned. Admiring it, she thought she too must have one, though it must be cheaper. Kezzie's daily cleaning woman had already been in and had gone, after putting out the things for coffee and biscuits. Tess was more than happy to keep her house clean herself, not liking or seeing the need for another woman about the place, though she paid Kezzie's gardener to do some work for her; John had always been the gardener and she had no ability for it.

Robert had banked for her what seemed an enormous sum, begging her to use it and get some pleasure out of life. Just the same, when Kezzie suggested they drove into Cheltenham to do a bit of shopping and have lunch there, Tess couldn't help feeling it was being extravagant. Kezzie noted her hesitancy. She at once stood her ground, saying, "I know it's cheaper to eat at home, and your Robert has told me how you've spent a lifetime trying to make a penny go as far as two. But there's no need of it any more. He wants you to have a very comfortable old age, and to have all the things you have never been able to have. Besides, I've got plenty of savings, and I can and will treat you sometimes. I've been all over the world, Tess, you've been nowhere and it would have been so wonderful if you could have shared it with me when we were both young enough to enjoy it. You really are the luckiest, though, getting married and having children. Now you could do me the greatest favour by coming with me on holiday and sharing the experience. Oh Tess, I was always so lonely in my heart!"

Tess at once gave in, feeling ashamed at her ungratefulness and at the way in which Kezzie expressed her loneliness. Having had a wonderful day trawling the shops and eating expensive meals, they came home from Cheltenham with a sheaf of holiday brochures, spending the evening working out future plans. The next afternoon, when they went for a walk in the Forest of Dean, there were long compatible silences. Life became a rich experience which their natural intelligence helped them savour to the full. They didn't always agree and had hard fought arguments without malice, putting their points of view with vigour. But they could also sit contentedly reading or napping off in each other's company

One day, as they meandered along a woodland path, Kezzie asked, "Do you sometimes wish you'd never grown up, Tess, that you still half-believed in fairies?"

Tess stood for a moment in thought before saying, "I don't really know, Kezz. Despite everything, John and the boys made it all worthwhile. It seems to me your life has been like a fairy story. Even when we used to talk all that childish prattle, we never dreamed up such fame and fortune. Do you miss the limelight, Kezz?"

"Sometimes, but I've had the glitter, you've had the gold, Tess. All the clapping and encores in the world won't equal the true love of one man," and she told Tess all about James Allison and Nigel Burke. So absorbed were they in each other's company and what had happened that only a desperate feeling of thirst and hunger brought them back to the moment.

"Good Lord, Tess, we've been walking for two and a half hours," exclaimed Kezzie, looking at her watch, "And I'm famished. We've come this far, so we might as well struggle on and go into the Speech House for a cuppa and something to eat."

"I've just realised my legs are killing me," grinned Tess. "Look at my varicose veins!"

"When we've eaten, I'll call a cab from the Speech House to take us home. That'll save your poor old legs from collapsing," suggested Kezzie.

"And I'll pay half," laughed Tess, with hardly a glimmer of guilt. The idea of going into a place like the Speech House to eat would have been unthinkable till now. She couldn't help being impressed by Kezzie's take-it-for-granted attitude. For Tess this was adventure, for Kezzie something mundane. But she thought she was beginning to understand what it really meant to have enough money.

The next day it rained all day, a good time, Kezzie thought, to go through the holiday brochures.

"How about four days in Venice?" Kezzie exclaimed after a while. "Do you remember how our teacher at school said it was one of the most beautiful places in the world? I was in Italy during the war but never went to Venice. It would be a real treat for me too."

"But we'd have to go on a ship and I can't swim!" demurred Tess.

"Oh Tess. Don't be silly. The English Channel is no distance. When you're out of sight of England, France is practically in view and besides, boats carry lifebelts. There's no risk and you'll love it. I'll arrange it all. You won't have to worry about a thing."

Tess's boys were enthusiastic about Kezzie's plans. It would be wonderful to hope Tess could be lifted out of her depression following John's death. Eventually Tess agreed to go, firmly suppressing her sense of panic.

The first morning of their holiday, she got up early, enamoured of Venice from their brief view of it on the previous evening. Kezzie was still asleep in one of the twin beds in the enormous and luxurious room they were sharing at the hotel. Quietly Tess went out in the morning air, loving the walk. When she turned to retrace her steps, she was overwhelmed with the beauty of the scene before her. The sunlight's reflections on the water, the blueness of the sky, the purity of the air and the noble architecture gave the view an ethereal quality. She stood letting it etch deeply in her memory to revisit in the future. She thought, "I must bring Kezzie here before breakfast". The company of Kezzie was a balm for the heartache of not having John with her

"So you like Venice then?" said Kezzie at breakfast

"Oh Kezz, I think it's absolutely beautiful!" she replied with a sigh.

Before they left the table, Kezzie was waving a roguish finger in front of Tess, saying, "Next year we'll go to America and visit my brothers. I haven't done that yet and they keep on at me to go."

Tess could think of no objection.

Life settled down for both, with a routine that most days they would go for a walk in the Forest, retracing the paths they had known as children and rediscovering the many little secrets they had had. At the same time, they shared each other's thoughts and memories, learning about each other's heartaches and joys. True to her word, the next summer Kezzie organised their trip to America, crossing the Atlantic on the *Queen Elizabeth*, with a cabin suite for the pair of them. Tess described the ship to her sons as like a floating posh hotel, and she was lucky enough never to be seasick, though Kezzie was sometimes. Kezzie's youngest brother met them in New York, in what Tess thought was a huge, opulent car. She soon realised it was the norm for most Americans, for there was plenty of elbow room and plentiful cheap petrol. The welcome they were given was wonderful and the hospitality of family and neighbours almost overwhelmed them. After experiencing the riches of New York itself, they were swept off to California, to stay with each member of the family in turn. They were amazed at the luxuries of American life, the air conditioning, the communal refrigeration plants for housewives to preserve their crops and poultry for a trifling rental, and the large unfenced lawned gardens. After the stringencies suffered during and after the war, and being naturally plain eaters, the amount of food offered almost horrified them.

On the way, Kezzie's brothers took them to visit the Grand Canyon. Awe-struck, they gazed into the enormous chasm.

"Brings us down to size, eh Tess? I feel like an insect!" commented Kezzie.

All too soon, their planned six week visit was over, and they returned to their beloved Forest, with a feast of memories to recall. Tess, impressed by the affluence of Kezzie's family, said one day, "Oh Kezz, it's wonderful how you have helped your brothers to get on," and she hugged her friend, who was trying to deny her responsibility.

From then on, it became usual for them to go off on holiday together, though never again as far as America. Kezzie, without a lot of resistance, took Tess to Spain, France and Portugal before the years began to reduce their stamina; then it was Scotland, Wales, Ireland and the Cotswolds. By the time her 80th birthday approached, Tess was a seasoned traveller. She could still manage to keep her own house clean, plant out her annuals in the flower borders and deadhead the flowers. Kezzie wasn't faring so well. She tried to make light of her failing mobility and odd aches and pains.

On the morning of Tess's 80th birthday, Robert and his wife surprised her by arriving at 10.00 am.

He hugged his mother, saying, "We're taking you and Kezzie out to lunch at the Speech House and then I've booked us all seats for J. B. Priestley's play *An Inspector Calls* in Cheltenham. Afterward we'll have dinner in the Queen's Hotel. Kezzie knows. I wrote and invited her to join us, and she's happy with the arrangements. And next Sunday Jim and his wife are coming up to take you both out for the day."

"Oh Rob!" and Tess buried her tearful face in his arms. They had a wonderful day out but, for Tess, it was overshadowed by her awareness that Kezzie seemed to be struggling to be her usual self. It was quite late before they were left on their own. "Kezz," said Tess in a manner that brooked no arguments, "you are going to the doctor's tomorrow, if I have to carry you there."

Kezzie unexpectedly did not argue. She sighed, and said, "It's my legs mostly, Tess, and my balance seems wrong and I feel funny in my head at times. It's just old age, I expect."

It was not old age. Despite Kezzie's dismissal of her symptoms, the doctor thought otherwise, and sent her to a consultant. There she was put through a series of tests. Before long, the news came through. Kezzie had something called Parkinson's Disease; there was no cure and it was a progressive illness. It was a terrible blow to them both. Almost in sympathy, rheumatism began to play up in Tess's joints. Neverthless, she spent her days in with Kezzie, doing everything she could for her comfort and, when Kezzie could manage with the help of a stick, going with her for little walks, sadly thinking back to the long days they had previously spent in their beloved Forest. They had enriched each other's lives, now they lived to bring what solace they could to each other. With Tess's encouragement and devotion, Kezzie struggled on for almost five years. She died peacefully one afternoon, slipping out of life while holding Tess's hand.

At the end, despite all of Tess's prejudice and Kezzie's pride, their lives had come together, surrounded by family and love. Childless, Kezzie had been adopted by and had adopted in spirit Tess's family, becoming a much-loved great aunt and great-great aunt to Tess's grandchildren and great-grandchildren. They all gathered to see her into her last home, and to help Tess over her second great loss.

But it was too much for Tess: with Kezzie's death her strength and the will to live had gone. She would sit looking into space for hours on end, her mind drearily half-empty. The house, though kept clean by her kind daily, began to look neglected while the garden ran to seed. Eventually, worried by her state of mind, Robert took her home to live with him but, despite all the encouragement of her loving family, Tess slipped away in the night a few months later.

Tess and Kezzie are buried near to each other, each with a fine headstone, in the churchyard where Tess helped to carry Kezzie's baby sister to her pauper's grave on the edge of the graveyard so many long years before.

Also available in ISIS Large Print:

Miss Bun, the Baker's Daughter

D. E. Stevenson

A masterpiece of light amusement from the remarkable D. E. Stevenson.

Sue Pringle shocks her family by her uncharacteristically impulsive decision to accept a post as housekeeper to Mr and Mrs Darnay, throwing their hopes of her marrying a local suitor into disarray. And then Mrs Darnay suddenly departs, leaving Sue's position in the house open for idle gossip — Mr Darnay is after all an artist, and everybody knows what that means. Oblivious to everyone's concern, Mr Darney and Miss Bun — as Mr Darnay has now re-named Sue — enjoy an easy working relationship. And it is not until Sue is summoned home that she finally realises the strength of her feelings towards her charming employer.

ISBN 0-7531-7083-3 (hb)
ISBN 0-7531-7084-1 (pb)

The Marigold Field

Diane Pearson

Through the vibrant years of the early part of the century — from 1896 to 1919 — lived the Whitmans, the Pritchards and the Dances, whose lives were destined to be intertwined . . .

Jonathan Whitman, his cousin Myra, Anne Louise Pritchard and the enormous Pritchard clan to which she belonged, saw the changing era and the incredible events of a passing age — an age of great poverty and great wealth, of the Boer War and social reform, of straw boaters, feather boas and the music hall.

Throughout all of this is the story of one woman's consuming love and of a jealous obsession that threatened to destroy the very man she adored.

ISBN 0-7531-7331-X (hb)
ISBN 0-7531-7332-8 (pb)

ISIS publish a wide range of books in large print, from fiction to biography. Any suggestions for books you would like to see in large print or audio are always welcome. Please send to the Editorial department at:

ISIS Publishing Ltd.
7 Centremead
Osney Mead
Oxford OX2 0ES
(01865) 250 333

A full list of titles is available free of charge from:
Ulverscroft large print books

(UK)
The Green
Bradgate Road, Anstey
Leicester LE7 7FU
Tel: (0116) 236 4325

(Australia)
P.O Box 953
Crows Nest
NSW 1585
Tel: (02) 9436 2622

(USA)
1881 Ridge Road
P.O Box 1230, West Seneca,
N.Y. 14224-1230
Tel: (716) 674 4270

(Canada)
P.O Box 80038
Burlington
Ontario L7L 6B1
Tel: (905) 637 8734

(New Zealand)
P.O Box 456
Feilding
Tel: (06) 323 6828

Details of **ISIS** complete and unabridged audio books are also available from these offices. Alternatively, contact your local library for details of their collection of **ISIS** large print and unabridged audio books.

1	21	41	61	81	101	121	141	161	181
2	22	42	62	82	102	122	142	162	182
3	23	43	63	83	103	123	143	163	183
4	24	44	64	84	104	124	144	164	184
5	25	45	65	85	105	125	145	165	185
6	26	46	66	86	106	126	146	166	186
7	27	47	67	87	107	127	147	167	187
8	28	48	68	88	108	128	148	168	188
9	29	49	69	89	109	(129)	149	169	189
10	30	50	70	90	110	130	150	170	190
11	31	51	71	91	111	131	151	171	191
12	32	52	72	92	112	132	152	172	192
13	33	53	73	93	113	133	153	173	193
14	34	54	74	94	114	134	154	174	194
15	(35)	55	75	95	115	135	155	175	195
16	36	56	76	96	116	136	156	176	196
17	37	57	77	97	117	137	157	177	197
18	38	58	78	98	118	138	158	178	198
19	39	59	79	99	119	139	159	179	199
20	40	60	80	100	120	140	160	180	200

201	211	221	231	241	251	261	271	281	291
202	212	222	232	242	252	262	272	282	292
203	213	223	233	243	253	263	273	283	293
204	214	224	234	244	254	264	274	284	294
205	215	225	235	245	255	265	275	285	295
206	216	226	236	246	256	266	276	286	296
207	217	227	237	247	257	267	277	287	297
208	218	228	238	248	258	268	278	288	298
209	219	229	239	249	259	269	279	289	299
210	220	230	240	250	260	270	280	290	300

301	310	319	328	337	346
302	311	320	329	338	347
303	312	321	330	339	348
304	313	322	331	340	349
305	314	323	332	341	350
306	315	324	333	342	
307	316	325	334	343	
308	317	326	335	344	
309	318	327	336	345	